AVOIDING COSTLY MISTAKES IN MARRIAGE

(+ over 70 prayer points to shield your marriage against destructive storms)

By: Simeon Medese

TABLE OF CONTENT

Foreword

The Biblical Facts About Marriage

The Common Mistakes:
#1 Inadequate Knowledge On The Subject Of Marriage
#2 Lack Of Appreciation
#3 Negative Mindset
#4 Dangerous Assumptions
#5 Unnecessary Aggression
#6 Inability To Understand The Nature Of The Opposite Gender
#7 Constant Unavailability
#8 Persistent Argument
#9 Baseless Accusations
#10 Temperamental Disparity
#11 Prolonged Asexuality
#12 Being Secretive To Each Other
#13 Personal Abuse
#14 Financial Abuse
#15 Relations Interference
#16 Health Neglect
#17 Insensitivity To Spouse's Needs
#18 Inability To Forgive
#19 The Act Of Infidelity
#20 Self Centeredness
#21 Ignoring Spouse's Voice
#22 Mr/Mrs Right Syndrome
#23 Nagging And Complaining
#24 Poor Communication
#25 Lack Of Mutual Respect
#26 Habitual Laziness
#27 The Nature Of Impatience
#28 Lack Of Commitment To Prayer

THE BIBLICAL FACTS ABOUT MARRIAGE

1. God is the originator of the marriage institution. And He made it a lifetime relationship between one man and one woman for mutual cohabitation, chastity, procreation and support.

"And he answered and said unto them, Have ye not read, that he which made them at the beginning made them male and female, And said, For this cause shall a man leave father and mother, and shall cleave to his wife: and they twain shall be one flesh? Wherefore they are no more twain, but one flesh. What therefore God hath joined together, let not man put asunder." Matthew 19:4-6 KJV

2. Marriage is a spiritual phenomenon, and it cannot be enjoyed in the divine context without a proper spiritual understanding and divine connection. You need God to get the good in marriage.

"I am the vine, ye are the branches: He that abideth in me, and I in him, the same bringeth forth much fruit: for without me ye can do nothing." John 15:5 KJV

3. There is no good or bad marriage anywhere, but two good or bad individuals make marriage whatever it becomes to them.

"Even so, every good tree bringeth forth good fruit; but a corrupt tree bringeth forth evil fruit. A good tree cannot bring forth evil fruit, neither can a corrupt tree bring forth good fruit." Matthew 7:17-18 KJV

4. Just like any physical building with a foundation, walls and a roof, marriage is a phenomenal building; that is why it is being referred to as "a home". The foundation you lay for your marriage determines its stand and durability.

"And every one that heareth these sayings of mine, and doeth them not, shall be likened unto a foolish man, which built his house upon the sand: And the rain descended, and the floods came, and the winds blew, and beat upon that house; and it fell: and great was the fall of it." Matthew 7:26-27 KJV.

5. There is no perfect marriage in life, but there are only graciously growing homes everywhere. There is nothing grace cannot do; if we allow it. Growing in grace is what you need for your marriage to be a heaven on earth.

"But grow in grace, and in the knowledge of our Lord and Saviour Jesus Christ. To him be glory both now and forever. Amen." 2 Peter 3:18 KJV.

6. That a marriage is cool and peaceful does not necessarily make it a perfect one. There are always rooms for improvement and development in every aspect of a man's life until death.

"But when that which is perfect is come, then that which is in part shall be done away. When I was a child, I spake as a child, I understood as a child, I thought as a child: but when I became a man, I put away childish things." 1 Corinthians 13:10-11 KJV

7. The school called 'marriage' never graduates any student but expels those who are unwilling to learn, pray and adjust their lifestyles to the rules of marital success. Such individuals find their way out through the road called 'divorce'; this is never the will of God for marriage.

"They say unto him, Why did Moses then command to give a writing of divorcement, and to put her away? He saith unto them, Moses because of the hardness of your hearts suffered you to put away your wives: but from the beginning, it was not so." Matthew 19:7-8 KJV

#1

INADEQUATE KNOWLEDGE ON THE SUBJECT OF MARRIAGE

"My people are destroyed for lack of knowledge: because thou hast rejected knowledge, I will also reject thee..." Hosea 4:6 KJV

Knowledge is the power for a real and fulfilled life. Ignorance is the surest dose to regret. Where knowledge is missing, an error is inevitable. Nothing can be better than having adequate knowledge about life itself, for fulfilment to be achieved in any sphere of it.

It is generally observed that the word 'marriage' is fast becoming a threat to or a taboo for many in societies today. While some married folks are on the search for the possible way out, many unmarried youths are full of questions that keep them at bay on this lifelong decision. Something must be wrong somewhere; in the beginning, it was not so.

The truth about this critical issue is that nothing is automatic in life. One thing leads to the other. The level of exposure acquired over an issue determines the degree of authority that can be exercised on it. It is sad to know that many people find themselves in marriage when they are neither mentally nor spiritually prepared for it. Many view marriage as a natural system that works for anyone that finds himself or herself in it. Some, on the other hand, see it as a culture imposed system of living, thereby running their homes at cultural or societal dictates. All these are the wrong ideas that lead to destructive mistakes in marriages today.

It must be clearly stated that marriage is a lifelong school of learning which requires a conscious effort for submission and loyalty daily. It is therefore very important for anyone who wants to succeed in marriage to willingly submit him or herself to continuous marriage education through books, sermons, counselling and marriage teaching materials; regardless of age, status, religious inclination, or class. This will empower and help in achieving marital success at large; whether married or single.

The following topics can serve as a guide of study for anyone who intends to build a successful marital life:

- How to pray through to know your right partner.
- Understanding a godly courtship system
- How to handle and relate well with the opposite gender.
- Effective communication in marriage.
- Maintaining good relationship with in-laws.
- Understanding temperaments.
- Financial management in marriage.
- Understanding parenting.
- Balancing career and marriage.
- Building a vibrant spiritual family life.
- And many more.

What you know is the platform that lifts you above the storms around. It is never late to learn, do it now.

PRAYER POINTS

1. Father, release upon me and my spouse the spirit of knowledge, wisdom and understanding for all-around excellence in life in the name of Jesus.

2. Every wrong step we have taken in life, that is responsible for one crisis or the other in our marriage now, Father Lord, help us out of it now by your mercy in the name of Jesus.

3. We receive the grace to conquer and succeed in marriage; in the name of Jesus.

#2

LACK OF APPRECIATION

"In everything give thanks: for this is the will of God in Christ Jesus concerning you."1 Thessalonians 5:18. KJV

Thanksgiving is one of the major secrets of success in life; while ungratefulness is a killer of good things, marriage inclusive. Every human being loves to be appreciated. No wonder William James, a renowned philosopher once said: *"the deepest principle of human nature is a craving to be appreciated*".

An unthankful husband or wife gradually suppresses the enthusiastic quest for good deeds in the spouse unknowingly.

Appreciation is a trigger for positive actions. It provokes right thinking, suggests positivity, lightens emotions and strengthens a relationship. Spouses need to be appreciative of every little effort made towards each other. They need to know they are appreciated for everything.

There are different modes of appreciation:

i. **VERBAL APPRECIATION:** This is the use of words to express a positive feeling towards a good deed of an individual.

ii. **NON-VERBAL APPRECIATION:** It is a positive action or expression in response to a good deed of an individual.

Spouses should adopt both verbal and non-verbal modes to appreciate themselves. Especially, the verbal mode should be generously used on a daily basis. This enables and assures the other party of being appreciated in an instant. Generally, women love verbal appreciation more. This will enhance positivity in their dealings and strengthen their love for each other.

Appreciation shouldn't be based on specific good deeds only but should be part of the norms in the home to always appreciate each other for being married together. Your spouse could have been someone else' partner, and you likewise. But for the love that subjected you both to tie the knot, you need to accord that great decision with daily appreciations.

Above all, couples need to constantly appreciate God for granting them the opportunity to be married; no matter the case.

John answered and said, A man can receive nothing, except it be given him from heaven. John 3:27 KJV

Every good thing is a privilege from above; it is not by human ability. Some of your mates, your older friends who may be more beautiful or more handsome than you are still on the praying altar for a marital breakthrough in life. Why not appreciate God always for making you a wife or a husband to somebody? Failure to show appreciation to God on behalf of your spouse constantly is also a great error that must be dealt with in marriage. Nomatter the case, God deserves to be appreciated always for everything. Remember, ***"In everything give thanks: for this is the will of God in Christ Jesus concerning you."***

Thanksgiving qualifies for a better end; it opens the door for the expected and the unexpected testimonies. It is the only form of prayer that exists in heaven. Use it as a tool to make your marriage a heaven on earth.

Prayer Points

1. Father I thank you, for giving me the privilege to be married in life in the name of Jesus.

2. Father Lord, forgive every attitude of ungratefulness in me and my spouse in the name of Jesus.

3. Spirit of Thanksgiving, come upon my life now in the name of Jesus.

4. Every good door that ingratitude has shut against my marriage, let the mercy of God open them to us now in the name of Jesus.

5. Let the reasons to continually thank God overtake my marriage permanently in the name of Jesus.

#3

NEGATIVE MINDSET

"For as he thinks in his heart, so is he" Proverbs 23:7 NKJV

The mind is a critical part of the body. It is the central controlling unit of all the human activities. In other words, the mind is the commanding officer that instructs the entire human body to act according to its dictates. Your mind is your master, where it goes you go. When the mind is wrongly set about an issue, the body cannot be rightly positioned about it. You are the product of your thoughts.

Some men get into marriage with a colonial slave master mentality, thereby, enslaving and mistreating their wives. Some women likewise, get married with the mind of liberty and a fantasy world. As a result, they waste every available resource in fashion making, partying and attending picnics all about. These kinds of mindset can hit the marriage against the rock or drown it in the sea of "had I known".

Until the mind is rightly informed, it will continue to produce a deformed life.

"...be ye transformed by the renewing of your mind..." Romans 12:2 KJV

Before going into marriage, you need to dissolve all wrong notions and ideas you've successfully gathered from your parents, family and friends about marriage; and feed your mind with the right definition of what marriage entails. The fact that your father was a bullying and a tyrannical husband to your mother does not mean that is the right way to treat a wife.

Also, that your mother was a career woman who was never available to cook, wash and cater for her home physically as expected under the disguise of busy work schedule or business activities, is not a standard or yardstick for you to operate as a wife. Your father or mother may do it and get on with it, but your spouse may not be at the same understanding and endurance level; hence, you find yourself to blame if you try it.

Many have ruined their marriages with the kind of mindset and philosophy they grew with as regards marriage. Some believe that no man can be trusted; hence, they live under the bondage of suspicion all day in marriage with a free and simple-hearted spouse who never sees anything to suspect even in a criminal; since God is on the throne.

MIND ANALYSIS

The human mind can be divided into three distinct functional segments which can be called the mind-wombs. They are:

i. Memory
ii. Contemplation
iii. Imagination.

The realm of memory contains the information of the past; contemplation handles the issues of the present; while imagination produces the future expectations. All unforgiveness, revenge, malice and bitterness are stored in the memory womb of the mind, and cannot lead to a better end if not reformed. For the imagination to produce a positive result, the memory needs to be properly sieved and refined through the womb of contemplation. This can only happen through books, sermons, teachings, counselling and other resources that supply the right information on the subject matter.

A negative mindset attracts a negative result no matter how prayerful one may be. Faith and doubt all proceed from the same heart. What you conceive within, you will conform to without.

Don't imagine any crises for yourself when it is not really there. Rather, you can program your life into a positive end through the positive thoughts you allow in your heart. Set your mind right about your spouse and you will see him or her responding to your positive imaginative dictates; thus, you will enjoy your marriage without any hitch. What you call your marriage within, I mean in your thought realm, is what it becomes in reality for the world to see.

Prayer Points

1. I cast out every power of negative imagination from my marriage now in the name of Jesus.
2. I receive the power for right and positive thinking now in the name of Jesus.
3. I bring to the obedience of Christ, every thought that concerns me and my household in the name of Jesus.
4. Every negative mindset that has settled within me and my spouse against each other, be flushed out now by the Holy Ghost power in the name of Jesus.

#4
DANGEROUS ASSUMPTIONS

"Beloved, believe not every spirit, but try the spirits whether they are of God..."1 John 4:1 KJV

To assume is to conceive a notion, premonition or mindset about an issue or an individual without a valid proof. In other words, it is a self-induced belief over a specific matter, a person or a situation without a cogent verification.

An assumption is the father of misinterpretation and confusion. To always assume is a dangerous ideology and philosophy that often leads to a catastrophic end; especially in marriage. To say the fact, the human heart is so deep than the deepest of all depths; and so unpredictable such that the owner of it may not be able to ascertain his next line of action when confronted with some unexpected situations. The Bible rightly says:

"The heart is deceitful above all things, and desperately wicked: who can know it?" Jeremiah 17:9 KJV

The truth remains that marriage is NOT a game of chances where things are undefined and left to occur at will. Rather, it is a world of reality where words, thoughts, actions and intentions are cautiously expressed regularly. It is a school of questioning and interrogations where responses are needed to every question from time to time. It is an atmosphere of deliberation and assertions so that life can be well spelt for necessary adjustment at every stage.

Before going into a marriage, wisdom requires that you spell out and define some things properly as much as possible based on your expectations; so that you don't get disappointed in the course of the journey. You need to define what marriage means to you and to your intending spouse. You need to define his or her physical, spiritual, and financial status.

Also, as a married man or woman, you have the divine mandate to constantly, check things out on your spouse as often as possible. Never assume anything but ensure the correctness of everything as much as possible and leave the rest to God.

Many ladies assumed wrongly that their intending husband was financially secured until they got married to realize that he was not only jobless but also a goalless individual without a dime in his savings. Some men likewise have fallen victim of assumptions, thinking that their intending wife was a well brought up homemaker; but to their amazement, such were later found to know next to nothing on domestic matters; starting from the kitchen to the bed. What a pity; an assumption is an error.

There are many married men and women who are in bitter pain of one assumption or the other about the man or the woman they've married today. My simple counsel to such individuals is to personally forgive themselves, discuss it with each other and pray for grace to handle the situation in a mature manner. Meeting a marriage counsellor is also a better option if the case appears difficult for them to handle.

The fact remains that the human heart is so deep and very unpredictable; so, here is my simple advice:

Never believe you know your spouse until he or she has proven himself or herself beyond every reasonable doubt. Events will surely unfold the real person you marry, and time will tell the real identity of the man or woman with whom you are going to spend the rest of your life. All you need is a little patience to decode some little steps that seem irrelevant.

For any marriage to thrive, flourish and be able to endure the test of time, every aspect must be properly cross-checked, accessed and thoroughly examined; not only at the foundational level but also on a daily basis all through life. This is not to be suspicious of each other but to fortify and strengthen daily the bond of trust for each other, as well as give room for improvement, development and a holistic growth in the family. The Holy Spirit is the principal actor in helping over this matter; give Him enough room to tell you all you need to know about your marriage life.

The secret things belong unto the Lord our God: but those things which are revealed belong unto us and to our children forever, that we may do all the words of this law. Deuteronomy 29:29 KJV

Howbeit when he, the Spirit of truth, is come, he will guide you into all truth: for he shall not speak of himself; but whatsoever he shall hear, that shall he speak: and he will shew you things to come. John 16:13 KJV

Prayer Points

1. O Lord my God, please, rebuild every broken edge of my marriage now in Jesus name.

2. Every mistake I have made in the past, that is currently having negative effects on my marriage, let them be reversed and be nullified now by the blood of Jesus in the name of Jesus.

3. I uproot and destroy every seed of error and mistake that have ever been sown into my marriage in the name of Jesus.

4. Every hidden information that the devil is using against the peace and the prosperity of my marriage, Holy Spirit, expose and resolve them now in the name of Jesus.

5. Every ancient hidden covenant of my family lineage that is working against my marriage, be nullified now by the blood of Jesus.

#5

UNNECESSARY AGGRESSION

"[Let] nothing [be done] through strife or vainglory; but in lowliness of mind let each esteem other better than themselves." Philippians 2:3 KJV

The word aggression can simply be defined as the feeling of anger or antipathy, resulting in hostile or violent behaviour in readiness to attack or confront. Simply put, aggression is a forceful reaction of self-defence.

Take note of these words: 'Forceful reaction' and 'self-defence'; they simply suggest 'danger'. This means that aggression is a dangerous act wherever it appears. Whatever is done aggressively saps some energy in the process. It never adds but takes away. It is a medium of minus or reduction of your peace and harmony in the home. You don't need to shout to be heard, neither do you need to yell to express your intention.

A professor of psychology in a lecture explained that it is not the physical distance that makes us shout at each other in the home, but the gap in the minds. The closer the hearts become to each other, the more calm and relaxed they are in their expressive deeds. This explains why shouting and bitter reactions are not generally associated with sexual moods since the two hearts are deeply and closely knitted in that brief moment.

The bible expressly commands:

Let nothing be done through strife or vainglory; but in lowliness of mind let each esteem other better than themselves. Philippians 2:3 KJV

Marriage is a system for mature minds and not for babies. Self-defence in marriage is an immature act to prove superiority over the other party. Be reminded that you are not in a contest or competition; however, you are in a deal of complementing each other; hence, needless is your self-defence act. The only person that needs your defence is your spouse. Please defend him or her for your bond to be stronger.

You cannot enjoy your marriage if you cannot defend your spouse. Even when he or she tends to do otherwise, there is always a better way to get things straightened.

The easiest way to overcome aggressive tendencies in marriage is by taking heed of Apostle Paul's counsel in the epistle to the Romans.

"...in honour, preferring one another". Romans 12:10b KJV

In other words, it means to deal with each other with honour, dignity, cordiality and respect; regardless of age disparity, educational differences, cultural background, societal stand or beliefs etc. Although it is commonly said that familiarity brings contempt, this does not apply to a God-fearing husband or wife; because the word of God is the binding force and the guiding manual for a godly marriage.

PRAYER POINT

1. Every arrow of bitterness, anger and disunity that has been assigned to work against my marital peace, I reverse and destroy them now in the name of Jesus.

2. Every negative character and misbehaviour in my life, be uprooted now by the power in the name of Jesus.

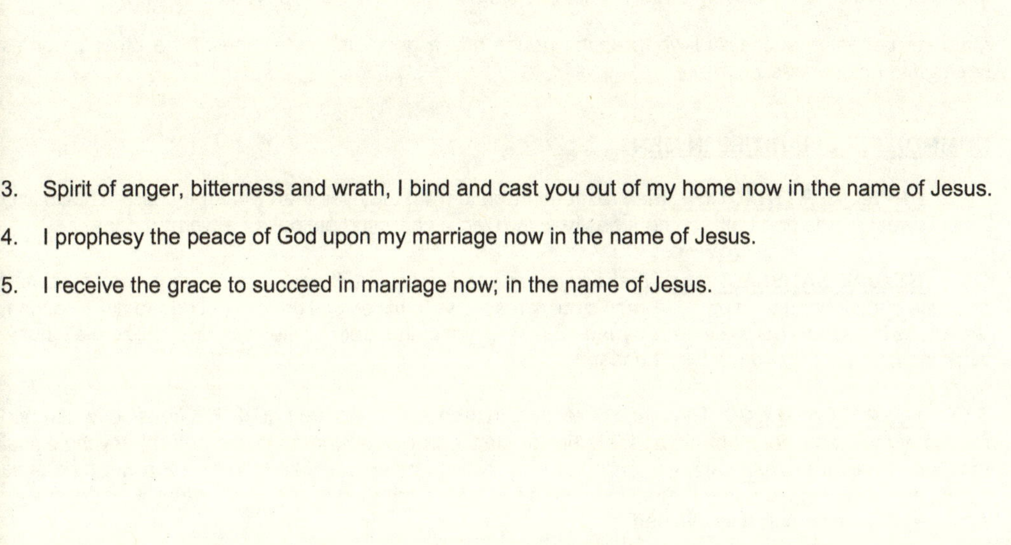

3. Spirit of anger, bitterness and wrath, I bind and cast you out of my home now in the name of Jesus.

4. I prophesy the peace of God upon my marriage now in the name of Jesus.

5. I receive the grace to succeed in marriage now; in the name of Jesus.

#6

INABILITY TO UNDERSTAND THE NATURE OF THE OPPOSITE GENDER

Likewise, ye husbands, dwell with [them] according to knowledge, giving honour unto the wife, as unto the weaker vessel, and as being heirs together of the grace of life; that your prayers be not hindered. 1 Peter 3:7 KJV

Knowledge is power, and what you don't know is beyond you. Until you discover it, you remain under its governing capacity.

Marriage is all about understanding. Failure to get this simple truth leads to outright marital failure.

We need to understand that God made us in the opposite gender in order to achieve unity in our diversity; it is not a mistake at all. We are meant to complement each other in all things.

There are some basic characteristics of each gender; also, their needs. Until you know who the opposite gender is, you cannot be a good spouse. You can't make your spouse happy if you don't know things that make him or her happy. In other words, you cannot solve the problem you don't know.

Marriage becomes successful when each spouse has a good understanding of the other person's needs and uniqueness.

COMMON PECULIARITIES IN MEN

1. **PHYSICAL ATTRACTION:** Men respond more to what they see than what they hear. That is why sweet words don't attract them easily. However, a charming outlook of a woman does.

2. **SEXUAL SATISFACTION:** What sex means to a man is different from what it is to a woman because of their gender disparity. A man's quick response to his sexual drive is not due to his emotional weakness but simply because he is a man. Starving him of this 'special diet' can destabilize his totality. Wise women don't do that to their husbands.

3. **RESPECT AND EGO:** The place of respect in men is a no-go area at all. His conscious demand for it is not just as a result of his age, stature or status; but as a function of his natural psychological makeup. An average man cannot withstand being insulted by his wife in any form; even when he sees no big deal in doing the same to her. Though this is totally wrong, it is one of the natural tendencies of a man that must be carefully avoided.

4. **SUPPORT:** A supportive wife is a great delight of her husband. Real men don't joke with this virtue. They love to be supported in achieving their dreams, pursuing their goals, making the home what it should be and help them to reach their desired end. That he is clamouring for her support is not as a result of his inability in pursuing that goal, but just a natural trait in him that makes him seek for a helpmate. God saw it in him even when he was unaware of it, that was why He said:

   "...I will make him an help meet for him" Genesis 2:18 KJV.

   Naturally, men need support, and they love it.

COMMON PECULIARITIES IN WOMEN

1. **ADMIRATION:** Unlike men, women are very sensitive to words. They are emotionally responsive to utterances. This answers why many of them are deceived easily by cheap vain promises of

some straying men. Women love to be admired; that is why they give it a lot to their loved ones especially when they are in a good mood. Praising and admiring your wife is a good tool for winning her love the more in marriage. Never castigate her publicly; it may cause a great damage to your marriage.

2. **Affection:** Women generally love to be treated with tenderness, love, care, physical touch, embrace, cuddle, etc. They value love and care in marriage more than men. The inability to get the needed affection can frustrate a woman out of her wedlock no-matter the available comfort.

3. **Conversation:** Women love talking, and they love to get people engaged with their talks. To keep the warmth in a marriage, the man needs to understand the talking spirit of the woman as one of her feminine qualities. Not for castigation or humiliation; but should help her channel her strength of speech in the right way and get her lively always.

4. **Security:** Every woman loves to be entrusted to a reliable and dependable man. She easily feels unsafe due to her weak nature; hence the need for a solace in the arms of a real man who is endowed with strength and agility. Her feeling of insecurity is not a problem but is due to her vulnerability as a weaker vessel. The presence of a man around her, therefore, gives a sense of great security in all dimensions.

5. **Dependability:** It is normal for a woman to look up to her husband for regular upkeep even when she is financially capable. It gives her a sense of satisfaction and fulfilment. Having this understanding makes the man undisturbed whenever she demands, especially when she has enough. She craves earnestly for trust and sincerity in helping her to rightly manage her strength, abilities and resources even when the man is not as buoyant as she is. The inability to meet up with bills, daily needs and truthfulness can weaken the love level of a woman.

You need to study your spouse the more and understand his or her peculiar tendencies. By doing this, you will know how best to relate to him or her always in order to achieve the best result in your marriage.

Prayer Points

1. Father Lord, give me the wisdom to relate to my spouse in her own uniqueness for success in our marriage in the name of Jesus.

2. My Father my God, destroy every negative tendency in my life that is capable of destroying my marriage in the name of Jesus.

3. Holy Spirit, take over the foundation of my marriage and rearrange it to glorify your name in the name of Jesus name.

#7

CONSTANT UNAVAILABILITY

"And the Lord God called unto Adam, and said unto him, Where [art] thou?" Genesis 3:9 KJV

Many couples today have failed to understand that the task of homemaking is a serious work that requires physical presence. Some have misplaced the order of priority by putting provision before presence. To provide the basic needs for the family is very good, but it cannot replace the physical presence of each family member. When the search for the daily bread denies your spouse and your children the pleasure of your physical presence, the end can be very dangerous and disastrous if care is not taken.

Generally, it is inadvisable for a husband or a wife to be engaged in a job or activities that perpetually steal away their presence from their home for a long period. No matter how good or genuine the excuse may appear, it usually has its negative effects on the home in the long run.

It was Adam's absence that opened the door for the serpent to deceive Mother Eve. Never open your matrimonial door to temptation or any sort of evil around. The great adversary of your peace is always lurking around seeking whom to devour. Therefore, be there physically to monitor and mentor every member to a fulfilling and successful end as divinely helped.

PRAYER POINTS

1. Any satanic personality that is declaring my position vacant in my marriage, I declare you paralysed and disgraced now by the Holy Ghost fire in the name of Jesus.

2. Every vacuum that has been, created knowingly or unknowingly in my marriage, be closed up now by the power in the blood of Jesus.

3. Every satanic attack against the unity of my household, I destroy them now in the name of Jesus.

4. Father Lord, baptise my family with the power of oneness in the name of Jesus.

5. Every good thing that has eluded my marriage in any form, be recovered for us now by the blood of Jesus, in the name of Jesus.

#8

PERSISTENT ARGUMENT

"Let all bitterness, and wrath, and anger, and clamour, and evil speaking, be put away from you, with all malice:" Ephesians 4:31

One of the dangerous traps that many couples fall into easily is the trap of argument. This usually occurs, as a result of contrary opinions or thoughts in the home. It is one of the most common devilish weapons that set the home in disarray if not managed properly.

We are not all the same; our principles, reasoning, philosophies, exposures and upbringing differ from each other. So, we are bound to have different views on issues sometimes. But our differences should not be placed above our common goal of marital success. We can always arrive at better results if wisdom and patience are allowed in our discussions.

THE DANGERS OF ARGUMENT

1.It creates a mood of temporary enmity.

2. It heightens emotions, tenses the muscles, increases blood pressure and can affect the entire body system.

3. It causes clumsy and irrational reasoning.

4. It creates a gap in the mind towards each other.

5. Sometimes, it leads to a temporary physical avoidance of each other.

6. Competitive thought that makes each individual to seek an upper hand of winning the argument.

7. It sometimes leads to physical fight or combat.

HOW TO HANDLE ARGUMENTS IN MARRIAGE

To overcome arguments in marriage requires a high level of maturity, patience, self-control, and humility which comes through the grace of God. It demands deliberate efforts by consciousness and self-discipline.

The following principles can always be of help if prayerfully adopted:

1. Be in charge of your mind and emotion no matter what the case may be. Don't lose control over yourself because of an issue. Your matrimonial relationship is more important than any point you are trying to make.

2. Think of your value for your spouse more than the issue causing the argument.

3. Be determined to retain your respect for him or her in the choice of your words no matter the mode of the argument. Avoid abusive and derogatory words.

4. Relax your muscles, especially the muscles around your mouth and eyes.

5. Breathe deeply. Clear the air emotionally by clearing the physical air in your lungs. It gives room for deep thought.

6. Change your focus within for a while. Focus on something other than what you are driving at.

7. Speak calmly at your lowest possible tone. If possible make your words few.

8. Allow time to interpret your points if you are still not being understood. You may leave the matter for a while and patiently bring it again at a better time and in a wiser way.

9. Evoke peace and laughter by causing a comic relief. Quickly think of something that will distract the hot mood and bring calmness.

10. Put on a smile, even if you have to force yourself to do so. Smile relaxes the emotion, brings affections, positive thoughts and feelings of gratitude.

11. Silence the grief by avoiding further thoughts about the issue or the person's reactions.

12. Always pray against the attack of the spirit of argument and misunderstanding in your marriage.

Prayer Points

1. Every argumentative spirit assigned against the peace of my home, I bind and paralyze you now in the name of Jesus.

2. Every negative tendency in me and in my spouse that is the opening door for satanic interference in my marriage, be destroyed now in the name of Jesus.

3. Spirit of wisdom and patience baptize me and my spouse now in the name of Jesus.

#9

BASELESS ACCUSATIONS

"Do not judge others, so that God will not judge you" Matthew 7:1 GNB

Every conflict is usually preceded by a form of alleging or accusation. Shifting blame is an immature act which depicts a sense of irresponsibility and often brings some forms of grudges, argument and schism in the home.

Taking responsibility for every error in the marriage is a great virtue of a real man and a real woman. This will always help you to avoid pointing accusing fingers at each other and you will always enjoy a friction-free atmosphere in your home.

When issues occur in the home, always take it upon yourself to ensure it does not lead to any argument or rancour. Rather, take the place of the wise gentle spouse who will always be willing to accept the blame for the error. This does not necessarily make you a fool but it shows you are a wise home builder.

The Bible admonishes thus:

Dearly beloved, avenge not yourselves, but rather give place unto wrath...Romans 12:19a KJV

Neither give place to the devil. Ephesians 4:27 KJV

PRAYER POINTS

1. Father Lord, fill my home with the fruits of the Spirit now in the name of Jesus.

2. My Father, my God, baptise my marriage with the spirit of wisdom to live peaceably always in the name of Jesus.

3. Father, let your love increase in our hearts daily that we may seek to please you and be like you in all things in the name of Jesus.

4. Whatever has been concluded in the coven of darkness over my marriage, I stand against it now and I destroy it totally in the name of Jesus.

5. Every unexplainable injury in the heart of my spouse that is dragging our marriage behind in life, be healed up now by the Holy Ghost in the name of Jesus.

6. O Lord, catapult my marriage to the mountain of fulfilment and perfection in the name of Jesus.

#10

TEMPERAMENTAL DISPARITY

So be careful how you live. Don't live like ignorant people, but like wise people. Ephesians 5:15 GNB

Every human being has a unique natural behavioural pattern. This is known as temperament. Your temperament is your nature, and your nature is the reason behind your actions and reactions. A good knowledge of the different temperamental characteristics will help you to understand yourself and your spouse better. It enables you to know how to deal with your weaknesses, as well as manage or maximize your strength and that of everyone around you for a better living.

The human psychologists have successfully grouped the different temperaments into four major categories namely:

i. Phlegmatic
ii. Sanguine
iii. Choleric
iv. Melancholy

These four general groups are subdivided into two groups, introvert and extrovert.

Apart from these four groups, there are several other blends or combinations which give us our individual behavioural brands. For example, **Phlegmel** is a combination of phlegmatic and melancholy, **Melsan** is a combination of melancholy and sanguine. **Chlorsan** means choleric and sanguine etc.

Each of these blends has its natural uniqueness in terms of strength and weaknesses. Some are of the introvert group while the others are of the extrovert group.

Whatever your temperamental makeup may be, it is not your making; just like you didn't choose your complexion, height or blood group. You were born the way you were made. Nevertheless, you hold the right to personally discover and work on your temperamental weaknesses; so that it does not affect your human and social interactions; especially, your relational life in marriage and other areas as well.

For instance, in a marriage between a melancholic wife (a critical and analytical introvert) and a sanguine husband (a free, funny and always assuming fellow), if the wife refuses to come out of her extreme introvert and perfectionist shell, she may end up frustrating her extrovert husband with untold loneliness and critical judgemental mood. This is a serious aspect of life that has led to many broken marriages in our society.

It is therefore very important for everyone to personally study and know more about the different temperaments and their individual peculiarities, so as to know how to help in developing a better behavioural pattern in marriage.

No matter how complex your blend and your weaknesses may be, the Holy Spirit is always available to help you reform and overcome in all things. Call upon Him and be open to His directives over it, you will surely become a better person in that marriage.

Howbeit when he, the Spirit of truth, is come, he will guide you into all truth: for he shall not speak of himself; but whatsoever he shall hear, [that] shall he speak: and he will shew you things to come. John 16:13 KJV

But the anointing which ye have received of him abideth in you, and ye need not that any man teach you: but as the same anointing teacheth you of all things, and is truth, and is no lie, and even as it hath taught you, ye shall abide in him. 1 John 2:27 KJV

PRAYER POINTS

1. Every negative attitude in my life, be uprooted and be destroyed now in the name of Jesus.

2. Every hidden battle that is waiting to disgrace me in marriage, be destroyed now by the Holy Ghost fire in the name of Jesus.

3. Every minus in my parent's marriage, become a plus in my marriage now in the name of Jesus.

4. Any satanic power that afflicted my parent in their marriage, shall NOT prosper over my marriage in the name of Jesus.

5. Holy Spirit divine, breath upon my marriage for excellence in the name of Jesus.

6. I receive the power and the wisdom to get it right in marriage in the name of Jesus.

#11

PROLONGED ASEXUALITY

"Do not deprive each other of sexual relations, unless you both agree to refrain from sexual intimacy for a limited time so you can give yourselves more completely to prayer. Afterward, you should come together again so that Satan won't be able to tempt you because of your lack of self-control." 1 Corinthians 7:5 NLT

Asexuality is a state of lack of sexual attraction or low sexual interest or desire in marriage. This may be due to many factors such as sickness, ageing, perpetual or persistent frictions, infidelity, distrust, spiritual attack, psychological defects etc.

Sex is a major function that must not be handled with any form of levity in marriage. It is the biological consummation of the marital relationship. It is also the climax of the emotional expression between a husband and a wife. Until sex is given its critical position in marriage, fulfilment will be outrightly impossible and fruitfulness will be a mirage or a shadow.

The Bible expressly commands:

"The husband should fulfill his wife's sexual needs, and the wife should fulfill her husband's needs. The wife gives authority over her body to her husband, and the husband gives authority over his body to his wife. Do not deprive each other of sexual relations, unless you both agree to refrain from sexual intimacy for a limited time so you can give yourselves more completely to prayer. Afterward, you should come together again so that Satan won't be able to tempt you because of your lack of self-control." 1 Corinthians 7:3-5 NLT

This scripture affirms the fact that sex is pivotal in marriage and it must not be for a selfish purpose. Rather, it must be for the satisfaction of the other party. When each of them seeks the satisfaction of the other party, they will both end in sexual satisfaction.

It is outrightly wrong to use sexual denial as a disciplinary measure for your spouse; especially when the basic needs are not met. It is a great sin to God and to yourself as a married person.

When a husband or a wife notices that his or her desire for sexual activity is gradually decreasing, the attention of the other party must be called to it, and both of them must find out the cause and quickly attend to it or adjust their matrimonial system.

Persistent asexuality or lack of physical affection will turn lovers into roommates, and this can trigger several other issues which can jeopardize matrimonial peace and harmony.

BENEFITS OF SEX IN MARRIAGE

1.It breeds purity

2. It is the highest level of godly pleasure

3. It is a form of communion

4. It is for marital stability

5. It helps to manage a crisis

6. It reduces tension

7. It improves immunity and a form of exercise

8. It increases intimacy

9. It makes women look younger and live longer

Prayer Points

1. Every satanic attack against my sexual life, be destroyed now in the name of Jesus.

2. Any evil personality appointed to monitor the sexual affair of my marriage, be arrested and be disgraced now by the Holy Ghost fire in the name of Jesus.

3. I declare the divine judgment against every satanic intercourse that is working against my marital peace, joy and harmony in the name of Jesus.

4. Any satanic arrow that has entered into my marriage through sexual sin, I declare the blood of Jesus against it, and I cast it out now in the name of Jesus.

#12

BEING SECRETIVE TO EACH OTHER

The man and the woman were both naked, but they were not embarrassed. Genesis 2:25 GNB

I recently heard the pathetic story of a man who was building a fantastic house somewhere at the outskirt of the city without the knowledge of his only wife but made it known to his bosom friend by keeping the document in his custody.

Unfortunately, he died before the completion of the project and the wife innocently stumbled on the detail in his diary. She confronted the so-called friend, but he denied the possession of the document, claiming that he only mentioned it to him without showing him the location. Such wife may struggle hard to overcome the sad memory of her late husband's distrust for the rest of her life, except for grace.

There is another funny incident of a wife who successfully built a house without the awareness of the husband. She connived with a caretaker to rent the same house to them when they had accommodation crises.

To worsen the case, she instructed the caretaker to exorbitantly increase the rent annually, while she also discouraged her husband from the idea of relocating each time he mentioned it. With her persistent apologetic plea, this simple-hearted husband continued to pay his 'landlady-wife' with the aim of making her happy since she claimed to like the house and the environment.

Like the scriptures rightly says, *"there is nothing hidden that will not be revealed" (Luke 8:17 ISV)* the innocent husband was busy tidying up the room one day when he stumbled on the hidden document of the building they were occupying with the name of his wonderful wife as the owner. You can guess what the end and the effect of that story will be on that marriage.

The problem of secrecy is one of the major challenges confronting marriages of our days.

"And they were both naked; the man and his wife, and were not ashamed" Genesis 2:25.

This shows that God's original plan for marriage is devoid of any secret between the husband and the wife. The man should see and know everything about the wife and vice versa in all things since they are both one flesh. But the devil, on the contrary, has successfully destroyed this principle in many homes by introducing double-dealing and privacy mentality. Some men have established a kingdom in a private room apart from their matrimonial room where they take solace and shelter from the 'interactive disturbances' of their wives. This is the beginning of gradual disintegration and indirect separation in that marriage.

There should be nothing like 'my room' or 'your room' in marriage. Although you can have a second room apart from your matrimonial room, which you can call any name of your choice; maybe study or prayer room. Both of you must have access to it for its designated usage and not a hideout for secret agenda; especially in times of little misunderstandings in the home.

Your mobile contact is registered in your name; agreed, but the phone belongs to both of you since you are one flesh. Hence, it has no information that your spouse cannot view at any time; otherwise, you are in a hidden deal that will jeopardize that marriage. When there is no skeleton in your wardrobe, openness cannot be an issue at all.

It is outrightly wrong to hide your information from your spouse. The end of it in many cases is usually disastrous.

Sadly, the system has degenerated drastically to the extent of a wife or a husband building or buying a property without the awareness of the other party. This is a technical way of disagreeing with God's principle of oneness and openness in marriage. In some cases, salaries, official benefits and even some biodata are kept secret from the spouses in the home. Imagine a husband hiding his real age from the wife or a wife not disclosing her real nativity to the husband. These kinds of attitudes have led to great losses in many families today. Many wives and children of some late rich husbands are struggling for daily survival at the demise of the men, simply because they kept their details from their spouses. Such wealth is being automatically inherited by the banks or the unfaithful hands to whom they have entrusted them.

The singular physical reason for these stories is distrust.

When trust is missing, marriage is gone. You cannot be entrusted to the one you cannot trust. If there is any virtue that needs to be restored into the marriages of today, it is no other but **TRUST**.

You should be able to prove your trustworthiness to your spouse and vice versa. This will curb the sin of secrecy and double-mindedness in your marriage. What God has joined together, let no room, phone, fund, sex, properties or person(s) put asunder. Under the normal circumstances, whatever belongs to you, belongs to your spouse. But perhaps you've been bitten and wounded by this evil monster of distrust, there is always a way out when you go to God for directives and wisdom on how to get things straightened up again. **SECRECY IS A SECRET DEMON THAT DESTROYS THE BEST OF ALL MARRIAGES; AVOID IT.**

PRAYER POINTS

1. Holy Spirit, repair all the broken edges in my marriage now in the name of Jesus.

2. Spirit of disagreement, I bind and I declare my marriage untouchable for you henceforth in the name of Jesus.

3. Every evil agreement that is working against the peace and the unity of my home, I command you to scatter now in the name of Jesus.

4. Every evil foundational power that has vowed to destroy my marriage, I command you to fail woefully and be disgraced now in the name of Jesus.

5. Holy Spirit, take your place in my household now in the name of Jesus.

#13

PERSONALITY ABUSE

"But if you act like wild animals, hurting and harming each other, then watch out, or you will completely destroy one another." Galatians 5:15 GNB

The act of slapping, spanking, beating, giving corporal punishment to your spouse is an abuse and an aberration that **MUST** be avoided at all cost in marriage.

Treating spouses like a slave and many other such shrewd acts are some of the common errors found in many marriages in the society today. This is ungodly and unethical. Your spouse is not your house-help or servant (even servants shouldn't be treated as such). So, don't treat him or her as one; no matter what the case may be.

The Bible admonishes us to cherish our spouses as we do to our own bodies.

"So ought men to love their wives as their own bodies. He that loveth his wife loveth himself. For no man ever yet hated his own flesh; but nourisheth and cherisheth it, even as the Lord the church: Nevertheless let every one of you in particular so love his wife even as himself; and the wife [see] that she reverence [her] husband." Eph 5:28-29,33 KJV

Husbands, love [your] wives, and be not bitter against them Col 3:19 KJV.

PRAYER POINTS

1. Every slavery mindset in me towards my spouse, and in my spouse towards me, be destroyed now in the name of Jesus.

2. Father Lord, give me a peaceful home till the end in the name of Jesus.

3. Father Lord, give me the grace to succeed in marriage in the name of Jesus.

#14

FINANCIAL ABUSE

Wise people live in wealth and luxury, but stupid people spend their money as fast as they get it. Proverbs 21:20 GNB

It has been observed that most marital frictions are often directly or indirectly finance related. Since money plays a major role in our day to day affairs, we cannot but face the fact that we need to give the right attention to the making and the management of it. When money is not judiciously utilized, it becomes financial abuse.

Financial issues, therefore, need to be properly discussed, and carefully handled on a regular basis in marriage, so as to avoid any form of mismanagement and abuse of funds. This will enhance financial trust for both parties, strengthen harmony, as well as build a worthy legacy for the children in the family.

Although there is no singular binding rule to financial management in marriage, truthfulness and openness is the surest key.

PRAYER POINTS

1. I stop every form of financial embarrassment around my marriage now in the name of Jesus.
2. I decree financial peace upon my marriage in the name of Jesus.
3. Every instrument of financial difficulty in my life and my marriage, be destroyed now in the name of Jesus.
4. My Father, My Father, release the wisdom for financial prosperity upon me and my spouse now in the name of Jesus.
5. Father Lord, rearrange our finances to the glory of your name in the name of Jesus.

#15

RELATIONS INTERFERENCE

"Therefore shall a man leave his father and his mother, and shall cleave unto his wife: and they shall be one flesh." Genesis 2:24 KJV

The bond of the marriage covenant is strictly for the husband and the wife.

This means that the parents, extended families and the relatives are all external parties that you need to **LEAVE** out of the scene of matrimony in order to be able to **CLEAVE** perfectly to your spouse. As such, they should **NOT** be given a higher priority over your spouse although they are **NOT** to be neglected.

Exposing the inadequacies of your spouse to your parents or siblings is a serious error that destroys marriage beyond imagination. As much as possible, never announce your matrimonial secrets to any third party; except in some extreme cases that may involve life threat.

PRAYER POINTS

1. Every anti-marriage family bond, that is holding me or my spouse down, break and be destroyed now in the name of Jesus.

2. Any assigned personality from any quarter, that is interfering with my marriage affair in order to destroy it, be arrested by the Holy Ghost fire and be disgraced now in the name of Jesus.

3. O God my Father, deliver my marriage from every evil family pattern in the name of Jesus.

4. Father Lord, build a wall of fire around my marriage against every form of satanic interference in the name of Jesus.

5. Every unfriendly friend around my marriage, be exposed, be disgraced and be separated from us now in the name of Jesus.

#16

HEALTH NEGLECT

Is there no medicine in Gilead? Are there no doctors there? Why, then, have my people not been healed? Jeremiah 8:22 GNB

Next to godliness in human life is sound health. When health is affected, almost everything stands still, including marital peace, joy, progress and prosperity. Love is put to test, and patience is often jeopardized in the days of health challenge. To say the fact, poor health is an arch enemy of the real life and marital bliss.

It is only a healthy man that can adequately attend to the physical, financial, emotional and even spiritual needs of his wife; so also it is with the woman. That is why the physical health of everyone in marriage should be given a maximum attention.

Unfortunately, many people prefer to invest in projects, parties, studies and other material things at the expense of their health care. **The truth is, the price of health neglect is far more than that of health care**. When the body is misused and left unattended to, in the pursuit of other goals, the result is usually devastating on whatever achievements are made.

One of the qualities of a wise couple is the ability to pay serious attention to the healthy living of every member of the family. **You don't need to be sick before rising to the task of health care. Rather, you are to aim at preventing ill health through what you eat and how you live on a daily basis. Remember, marriage can only be enjoyed by a healthy body**.

PRAYER POINTS

1. I declare my marriage exempted from every form of sickness and infirmity in the name of Jesus.

2. Any hidden sickness in my body and that of my spouse, that is waiting for an appointed time in order to destroy my marriage, be uprooted and be destroyed now in the name of Jesus.

3. I receive the wisdom to eat and live right in order to avoid sickness in my life in the name of Jesus.

4. Anything I have done in the past, that has given a legal ground to any sickness in my life, be nullified now by the blood of Jesus in the name of Jesus.

5. Let the Balm of Gilead (the blood of Jesus), take over the health affair of my household now in the name of Jesus.

#17

INSENSITIVITY TO SPOUSE'S NEEDS

(If you value someone, express it when needed)

[Be] kindly affectioned one to another with brotherly love; in honour preferring one another; Romans 12:10 KJV

The human nature is wired in a way that makes us to always be in need of one thing or the other all through life. Everyone always needs something, and no one needs nothing. A need is like a vacuum that yearns for a filling.

When there is a need, the first thing that comes to mind is 'who' can meet this need. Every need is attached to a 'who' i.e. a person.

One of the purposes for marriage is to avail humanity the 'first aid personnel' for every 'need vacuum'. That is to say, that marriage is designed to solve the problem of need in humanity. To every individual, there is a specific kind of the opposite gender that is naturally endowed with the ability to meet this need. In other words, every husband is a solution to his wife; and every wife is a solution to her husband.

The first challenge is the inability to know the need of your spouse. You cannot solve a problem you don't know. You need to know the physical, psychological, social, financial, emotional and the spiritual needs of your spouse; and then, you must be readily available to attend to these needs as much as lie within your capacity. The man should always be there to share the burden of need or pain with the woman, while the woman also does likewise in meeting the needs for the man; hence, the term "a help meet". This symbiotic living is one of the sources of the real marital joy and fulfilment. Anything short of this is a path to marital failure.

It is, therefore, a serious crime for a husband or a wife to be nonchalant and insensitive to the physical, spiritual, emotional and financial needs of his or her spouse. This is one of the causes of broken marriages in the society today.

Remember, the value you place on your spouse determines the treatment you give him or her.

PRAYER POINTS

1. Any form of difficulty and challenge confronting my marriage now, become a stepping stone now in the name of Jesus.

2. O God my father, manifest your power over every unpleasant situation surrounding my marriage now in the name of Jesus.

3. Holy Spirit divine, fill every vacuum in my home with uncommon testimony in the name of Jesus.

#18

INABILITY TO FORGIVE

And be ye kind one to another, tenderhearted, forgiving one another, even as God for Christ's sake hath forgiven you. Ephesians 4:32 KJV

The issue of unforgiveness is one of the greatest challenges in many marriages today. Many beautiful homes have suddenly been struck by this destructive trait, thereby leaving them in disarray.

An offence is a personal perception and view of people's actions. The inability to let go of offences is a critical trait that generates the seed of unforgiveness in the heart.

Bitterness is a piercing sword that tears the mind apart and binds the entire body, spirit and soul from real freedom.

Failure to forgive your spouse is tantamount to holding yourself down in bondage since both of you are one flesh. Forgiveness is not optional but mandatory for anyone who wants to enjoy the peace of life both physically and spiritually.

Moreso, forgiveness is the principal key to gain access to heaven in eternity. An unforgiving man or woman has no place in heaven but will have his or her final abode with the devil in hell forever.

So, if you don't want to forgive your spouse for marriage sake, why don't you do, for the eternal rescue of your own soul.

PRAYER POINTS

1. Every seed of bitterness in my life, be uprooted now by the blood of Jesus.
2. Any battle in my marriage as a result of grieve and bitterness, be nullified now by the blood of Jesus.
3. Wherever I have allowed my emotion to open door of attack to my marriage, Father Lord, deliver me by your mercy in the name of Jesus.
4. Holy Spirit, take over my thoughts, emotion and imaginations for your glory in the name of Jesus.

#19

THE ACT OF INFIDELITY

Since you are God's people, it is not right that any matters of sexual immorality or indecency or greed should even be mentioned among you. Ephesians 5:3 GNB

Marital infidelity is one of the major tools the devil uses to destroy a marriage and every good thing that surrounds it.

It is a great sin to God, to your spouse and to the children in that marriage. The consequence of marital infidelity is transgenerational; hence, it must be avoided at all cost.

Infidelity includes any form of immoral relationship with any other person apart from your spouse.

Don't you know that people who are unjust won't inherit God's kingdom? Don't be deceived. Those who are sexually immoral, those who worship false gods, adulterers, both participants in same-sex intercourse. 1 Corinthians 6:9 CEB

PRAYER POINTS

1. Any attack of immorality that is targeting my marriage for destruction, it shall not prosper in the name of Jesus.
2. Any satanic agent assigned to my marriage for any evil mission, be arrested, exposed and be disgraced now in the name of Jesus.
3. I secure my marriage with the spirit of righteousness now and forever in the name of Jesus.

#20

SELF CENTREDNESS

Let every one of us please his neighbour for his good to edification. For even Christ pleased not himself...Romans 15:2-3 KJV

The problem of 'self' is an ancient battle of the human race. It is the origin of all friction, rebellion and all forms of catastrophes on earth. Self is the inward suggestion that makes one's ego and positions a major issue of concern. It is the power that demands subjection at all costs but is never willing to subjects to anyone.

It is an internal force that sometimes manifests in form of superiority complex in some, and sometimes as an inferiority complex in others. It is the natural human tendency to feel cheated or to cheat on the other persons' simplicity.

To be self-centred in marriage is a serious problem that leads to the lack of consideration and understanding for the other person. It makes one excessively demanding for personal attention. It brings the feeling of insecurity and suspicion. If not properly handled, it leads to depression and marital frustration.

For any marriage to be enjoyable and fulfil the divine purpose, the place of self in each individual must be totally handed over to Christ for a total transformation of the inward man.

The Holy Spirit also must be given full allowance to rule and reign over the human emotion; thereby making the natural man loving, simple, submissive and full of the fruits of the Spirit.

This brings about selflessness, which is the opposite of self-centeredness. It gives the ability to forego one's personal comfort and satisfaction in order to attend to the need of the other person. It brings the quest for a price than the hunger for gain. Sacrifice, therefore, replaces self-satisfaction. In fact, value to add takes over the reward to receive. The thought of making him or her happy at all cost fills your heart always.

Of course, love becomes natural, and submission becomes easy in a marriage of a selfless couple.

Pray for it, work towards it and you will achieve it by His grace.

PRAYER POINTS

1. Every activity of 'Self' in my life, be arrested and be destroyed now in the name of Jesus.

2. Holy Spirit divine take over my emotion and transform it to your taste now in the name of Jesus.

3. Wherever I'm getting it wrong in my marital relationship, Father Lord, take me over and help me to get it right in the name of Jesus.

#21

IGNORING SPOUSE'S VOICE

"The way of a fool is right in his own eyes, But a wise man is he who listens to counsel." Proverbs 12:15 NASB

Everything in life has a voice, including your marriage. The more you refuse to listen to the voice at home (I mean your spouse), the more ignorant you become of the prevailing situations; and the more you gradually kill that marriage. Until you understand the voice within your bedchamber, you cannot enjoy the peace of the person therein.

Listening is a deliberate act that requires a concerted effort of the listener. It is also a time taken duty for everyone who wants to enjoy marital bliss. You cannot know what he or she is going through at a particular time if you cannot make time to listen to both the audible and the unproduced sounds in that union.

Communication is a duo game between a sender and a receiver, of a message.

There are two types of listening namely, the receptive and the defensive listening.

Receptive listening is the act of listening with the aim of understanding the mind and the mood of the speaker in order to know the right action to take; While the defensive listening is the attitude of listening to give a response that protects ego and self-image, not minding its relevance or effect on the message or the speaker. While the former talks about the solution, the latter thinks about the status of being right.

Defensive listening leads a marriage nowhere other than a frustrating end and divorce, but receptive listening moves the home to a better bonding and a harmonious end.

What kind of listening act are you fond of? If the wrong one, you need to make amend and adjust now before it is too late.

The beauty of marriage is greatly hidden in the depth of understanding each other's voice in whatever tone.

You need to study the best way to communicate your spouse in order to get your messages across. So also, you need to study to listen to your spouse 'in all good things' so as to walk in the unity of voice and purpose to a successful end. This will be a good virtue and a great legacy to leave for your children in life.

PRAYER POINTS

1. Every strange voice that is speaking in the foundation of my marriage, be silenced now by the blood of Jesus.

2. Every demonic interpreter of my voice in my wife's (husband's) ears, I bind, arrest and cast you out of my marriage now in the name of Jesus.

3. Holy Spirit, take over the communication affair of my home now in the name of Jesus.

4. My marriage shall prosper in all dimension in the name of Jesus.

5. I receive the utterance to speak right in my marriage in the name of Jesus.

6. Father Lord, fill me with the spirit of patience to act right always in the name of Jesus.

#22

MR/MRS RIGHT SYNDROME

"Never let yourself think that you are wiser than you are; simply obey the LORD and refuse to do wrong." Proverbs 3:7 GNB

One of the common characteristics of a good marriage is the ability to disagree to agree without any resentment or selfish interest. Amicably arriving at a result oriented compromise should always be the common goal; knowing fully well that it is impossible for you to always be right in issues at home. If you try, you may win the battle, but lose the war!

The Bible says:

Live in harmony with each other. Don't be too proud to enjoy the company of ordinary people. And don't think you know it all! Romans 12:16 NLT

Endeavour not to always have the last word. Admit when you make a mistake and believe that you don't have all the answers. Every couple needs to be able to handle conflict in a constructive way. Having an angry outburst so that you can win an argument will make you the loser in the end.

PRAYER POINTS

1. I decree the spirit of total humility upon my marriage now in the name of Jesus.

2. I take authority over every argument spirit in my marriage now in the name of Jesus.

3. Let the wisdom of God for marital success come upon my marriage now in the name of Jesus.

4. Wherever I have missed in time past, that is having a negative effect on my marriage now, let the mercy of God locate it and repair it now in the name of Jesus.

#23

NAGGING AND COMPLAINING

"We must not complain, as some of them did — and they were destroyed by the Angel of Death." 1 Corinthians 10:10 GNB

The word nag can be defined as an annoying or irritating attitude caused by persistent fault-finding, complain, or demand. It is a persistent expression of displeasure over a specific issue or different issues. Nagging and bitterness are close associates that affect good mood and relationship negatively. It is one bad trait that never allows continuous peace, joy and harmony in a marriage.

Being able to overlook some flaws and mistakes in your spouse is a sign of maturity in marriage. A repetitive announcement of the same issue without proffering a definite solution may sometimes make the home boring to a gentleman or simple-hearted wife. It is good to observe a fault, but it is better to devise a means to a realistic solution.

When a fault or a wrong deed is observed in marriage, the first thought that should come to mind is: "what is the best approach to achieve the best result?" This approach should aim at avoiding any form of grieve in the other party. Carefully, lovingly and calmly making the point clearly known will naturally give the desired result. By so doing, the observed fault will not be seen as a complaint, but an issue that needs to be corrected or adjusted. Your marital relationship is of a higher value than any personal opinion. Treat it carefully, with all dignity.

Nagging destroys marriage, avoid it.

PRAYER POINT

1. Every temperamental weakness in me and my spouse, holy spirit empower us to conquer them now in the name of Jesus.

2. I submit my thoughts and my emotion to the power of the holy spirit now in the name of Jesus.

3. I receive the grace to live a peaceful life with everyone around me in the name of Jesus.

#24

POOR COMMUNICATION

"Let your speech at all times be gracious and pleasant, seasoned with salt, so that you will know how to answer each one [who questions you]." Colossians 4:6 AMP

Communication is the starting point as well as the sustaining strength of every relationship. Understanding communication makes a good and sustainable fellowship. Effective communication makes an effective team; thereby making goals achievable and visions realistic.

When the wall of communication is cracked in a marriage, things automatically fall apart. Many divorced cases would have been simply avoided only if the wall of communication had been well guarded. Many battered marriages would have been made better if they had only mastered the art of effective communication in marriage.

Unfortunately, many Christian marriages are not left out of the pain and the wound of poor communication, due to their ignorance of the danger that lies ahead if due attention is not given to this aspect of marriage.

Communication in marriage goes beyond a mere talk and response system. It is the central point of the relational life. The binding force that glues the hearts together and as well the breaking tool that sets each apart. It is a school that must be mastered in order to enjoy marriage on earth.

CAUSES OF POOR COMMUNICATION IN MARRIAGE

1. Pride, the thought of self-sufficiency and self-consciousness.
2. Lack of self-confidence.
3. Distrust and insincerity.
4. Language limitation.
5. Wrong mindset.
6. Absent-mindedness.
7. Ignorance of love languages.
8. Impatience
9. Poor listening skill.
10. Bitterness, malice and unforgiveness.
11. Lack of empathy.
12. Spiritual attack

DANGERS OF POOR COMMUNICATION IN MARRIAGE

1. It causes emotional trauma.

2. It exposes marriage to external interference.

3. It affects sexual intimacy.

4. It weakens the marital bond.

5. It weakens spirituality

6. It hinders answer to prayer

7. It causes health crises

8. It can lead to death.

GOLDEN RULES FOR EFFECTIVE COMMUNICATION IN MARRIAGE

1. Always maintain a more conducive atmosphere for a free flow of information between both of you.

2. Be open-minded, don't be secretive.

3. Avoid an aggressive or militant facial look always.

4. Be sensitive to your spouse's body languages and mind the expressive movements as applied.

5. Cultivate the act of intentional listening. Do not simply hear the words spoken, but show that you are actively engaged in conversations with your spouse.

6. Always avoid wandering thought during a discussion with your spouse; deliberately participate in his or her speech by absolute concentration.

7. Consciously give a response of hope and assurance even when a definite solution is not yet coming to mind.

8. Avoid every form of distraction and interruption. Paying more attention to the mobile phone, or a computer or television set is unethical in your talk times.

9. Avoid assumption of understanding, don't expect your spouse to be a mind reader, be clear with your points.

10. Never sleep over any misunderstanding; resolve it instantly and keep your love fire burning.

11. Always pray about your communication life and study to improve on it.

PRAYER POINTS

1. Every satanic power that is interfering in the communication affair of my marriage be paralysed now in the name of Jesus.

2. Voices of darkness that are speaking against my voice in my husband's/wife's ear, be silenced forever now in the name of Jesus.

3. Holy Spirit divine, take over the communication life of my marriage now in the name of Jesus.

4. Wisdom for effective communication in marriage, come upon my life now in the name of Jesus.

#25

LACK OF MUTUAL RESPECT

"So then, in everything treat others the same way you want them to treat you, for this is [the essence of] the Law and the [writings of the] Prophets. Matthew 7:12 AMP

One of the common misconceptions in our days is the school of thought that says familiarity brings contempt. To a large extent, this may be proven to be right from the general day to day experiences. But in the real sense, it is an act of negligence towards our relational life; especially when we get so fond of ourselves.

Value accords respect. The degree of value attached to a person determines the degree of respect he or she is given. The boss at work or the pastor in the church is often highly respected not because he is not so familiar to us, but because he is of high value to us, thus held in high esteem; maybe for the salary he pays, or for the anointed prayers and prophecies he offers. If the marital relationship is valued, it should be treated with high respect likewise. This makes the marriage more meaningful and more productive. The value you attach to your spouse determines the treatment you give him or her.

Although the definition of respect differs from one culture to the other, the general interpretation and application of it at any time anywhere is simply to treat each other with honour and dignity.

[Be] kindly affectioned one to another with brotherly love; in honour preferring one another; Romans 12:10 KJV

This means that the man gives a respectful treatment to the woman always, and she does likewise.

There are different kinds of respects as seen today.

1. **PARTIAL RESPECT:** This is the kind of respect that is given only when things are good; either financially, physically, health-wise or otherwise. The moment the goodies of life are not coming as expected, respect is withdrawn from the table. This can also be termed a conditional respect. This is ungodly and satanic. It can be highly frustrating. It simply connotes carnality, greed and selfishness. It should be outrightly avoided in a Christian marriage.

2. **ONE-SIDED RESPECT:** This is the idea that sees respect as a duty and responsibility of only one party in the marriage. Most especially, in cultures that see the woman as a lesser person. Although the Bible commands the woman to be submitted to the man, this does not relegate her to a lower status. It rather suggests the order of authority in the home. She is to be treated as a dignified personality, to whom the entire home keeping affair is committed. She is a stakeholder and not a lesser partner. Remember, the scripture says "...in honour preferring one another". You must prefer her in honour, she must prefer you in honour too. Then God is glorified.

3. **HYPOCRITICAL RESPECT:** This is a system of respect that is not from the heart but just for eye service as a form of showmanship. It is rather a film trick or a dramatic display kind of respect in marriage. The danger of hypocritical respect is that it lacks genuineness and sincerity. Hence, it cannot stand the test of time; the human nature will definitely outburst at any time. It is a rebellion breeding respect.

More so, this kind of respect cannot yield the spiritual fruit of godliness that attracts the result of divine blessing that comes upon those who obey the word of God.

And whatsoever ye do [it] heartily, as to the Lord, and not unto men. Knowing that of the Lord ye shall receive the reward of the inheritance: for ye serve the Lord Christ. Colossians 3:23-24. KJV

4. **MUTUAL AND HOLISTIC RESPECT:** This is the kind of respect demonstrated in the marriage between father Abraham and his wife Sarah.

"Even as Sara obeyed Abraham, calling him lord: whose daughters ye are, as long as ye do well, and are not afraid with any amazement. Likewise, ye husbands, dwell with [them] according to knowledge, giving honour unto the wife, as unto the weaker vessel, and as being heirs together of the grace of life; that your prayers be not hindered."1 Peter 3:6-7 KJV

This is a wholehearted sincere godly respect, which is absolutely based on the love of God, His word and a godly love for one's spouse. It is selfless and sacrificial in nature. It has no gender disparity, cultural limitation or financial consideration. It is truthful and humble.

Let it be clearly stated at this point that the respect given in a Christian marriage is not for your spouse only, but for the authority of the word of God that binds you together. So, it must be handled carefully as unto the Lord.

Any marriage that lacks mutual and holistic respect needs prayers for the grace to possess this virtue.

PRAYER POINTS

1. I cast out every seed of arrogant and pride from my marriage now in the name of Jesus.
2. Father Lord, baptise my marriage with the spirit of humility in the name of Jesus.
3. Father Lord, fill marriage with the spirit of wisdom and submission in the name of Jesus

#26

HABITUAL LAZINESS

"If you are lazy, you will never get what you are after, but if you work hard, you will get a fortune." Proverbs 12:27 GNB

Many singles fail to realize that marriage is a serious work until they get married to find themselves at the centre of so many domestic demands. There will always be unavoidable payment of bills on a regular basis, house chores that must be attended to on daily basis, children that need to be catered for, and many other inevitable demands that require physical, psychological, emotional, financial and even spiritual strength, for marriage to be at its best. Failure to arise to these compulsory tasks can spell the doom for any marriage.

Laziness can simply be defined as the unwillingness to work, or to be active; either physically or mentally. It is a deliberate act of negligence to duties as demanded. It is the unwillingness to exert energy over a given task. Laziness is the direct enemy of success.

The disease called laziness is more destructive to any aspect of life than anything. It keeps the poor in his poverty, turns the rich towards the shadow of his reality, renders greatness useless, wastes great opportunities and destroys good links and fortunes.

A lazy wife always shifts her legitimate domestic duties to any available hand in her bid for comfort and satisfaction, not minding the outcome and the adverse effect on her home. So also, a lazy husband deliberately ignores his manly duties in marriage and subjects his family to unnecessary hardship as a result of his unwillingness to explore the field of labour.

Laziness prioritizes comfort over labour. It admires good things but hates the pain that gives birth to them. It loves harvest but detests cultivation. Treasures prize, but avoids price. Unfortunately, the word lazy is a negative word that no one loves to be associated with; even the lazy man does not want to be called lazy.

THE NEGATIVE EFFECTS OF LAZINESS IN MARRIAGE

1. Poverty and lack.
2. Waste of resources.
3. Limits exposure.
4. Kills targets and destroys projects.
5. Stagnates visions and hinders progress.
6. Turns one to a nuisance.
7. Overburdens the spouse.

HOW TO OVERCOME LAZINESS IN MARRIAGE

Overcoming laziness is a matter of personal determination. It requires consciousness of this destructive weakness, and the willingness to come off it at all cost.

To help yourself:

1. Be conscious of it and be smart to deal with it always in your life and marriage.

2. Constantly remind yourself of the harm it has done to you in the past, as well as the danger that lies ahead in the future if it is not destroyed now.

3. Develop an interest in hard work.

4. Voluntarily, submit yourself to be monitored by someone you hold in high esteem; preferably your spouse, and be accountable to him or her daily.

5. Deliberately, get yourself engaged in the tasks you naturally find boring or humiliating to you and be determined to conquer them yourself. Don't delegate them. Do it as a surprise to your spouse.

6. Be committed to duties and responsibilities always in order to avoid idleness at all time.

7. Monitor, regulate and maximize your rest and relaxation time strictly and judiciously.

8. Be time conscious of your tasks.

9. Always set a goal for things to be accomplished within a stipulated time. And work towards beating your goals always.

10. Wage war against procrastination, and cultivate the habit of "Do it now and do it well in order to get it right."

11. Pray for a 'never give up spirit' and never complain about duties, but face them to finish.

12. Cast out the spirit of laziness from your life until you see yourself being free from its activities.

PRAYER POINTS

1. I cast out every spirit of laziness from my life now in the name of Jesus.

2. Every good thing I have lost to the enemy as a result of my attitude of laziness in my life, O God, please recover them for me now in the name of Jesus.

3. Effort frustrating powers assigned to frustrate my ventures in life, I command you to be frustrated now in the name of Jesus.

4. Holy Spirit, empower me with fresh inspirations and ideas that will glorify your name alone in the name of Jesus.

#27

THE NATURE OF IMPATIENCE

Patience leads to abundant understanding, but impatience leads to stupid mistakes. Proverbs 14:29 CEB

The virtue of patience is an inevitable quality to any successful achievement in life. It is the ability to wait without becoming anxious or annoyed. It also means being calm and composed instead of being hasty or impulsive at issues or with people. Being patient is to be composed of understanding for a person or a situation. It makes one able to endure during pain or provocation. The more patient you are with others, the more positive view people have of you.

Impatience is the product of the fear of failure or the thought of missing it at one point or the other. It is a reaction that comes as a result of anxiety and nervousness over an issue. It is a negative mood that is often characterised by short breath, muscle tension, restlessness, irritability, anger and clumsy thoughts. Impatience is an attitude that must be carefully handled and avoided in anyone who aims at succeeding in life. More especially in marriage, a high degree of patience is required by each of the parties in order for them to achieve a good end.

THE DANGERS OF IMPATIENCE IN MARRIAGE

The pain of enduring patience is better than the regret of an impatient lifestyle. The absence of patience in marriage is a sure path to marital frustration and partial or absolute divorce. An impatient spouse is prone to the following errors:

1. Hasty and unreasonable resolutions.
2. Making rash decisions with terrible consequences.
3. A life of perpetual regret.
4. Aggressiveness instead of assertiveness.
5. A suspicious life, he or she lacks trust and double deals with the spouse.
6. Increased stress level which can cause physical harm to the bodies.
7. Uninformed about the spouse.
8. Unable to keep secrets.
9. Having negative views on issues rather than enjoying their positive ends.
10. Unable to bear with the spouse's weaknesses.
11. Damaged relationships.
12. Lacks focus and perseverance in pursuing a goal to its accomplishment; especially if the goal appears challenging.

HOW TO OVERCOME IMPATIENCE

Impatience is often traced to temperamental weakness or lack of emotional maturity. To overcome it requires a lot of conscious effort by the victim. This will enable him to work on it as well as pray until the Holy Spirit helps in conquering the syndrome.

The following practical steps can also help out:

1. Always take time to think through before speaking or acting.

2. Consciously delay to thoroughly verify issues before arriving at conclusion.

3. Since impatience is the product of the fear of failure, always assure yourself of a positive end to all your ventures in life. Develop a life full of faith and always work towards your goals systematically.

4. Endeavour to always focus on the **NOW**; think of how precious the present moment is to your successful life. Live a day at a time.

5. Always avoid a crash or a short route system to getting things done; except when you are very sure of its necessity.

6. Learn to always control your emotions. You have a choice in how you react to every situation.

7. Practice active listening and empathic listening. Make sure you give your spouse your full attention, and patiently plan your response.

8. Always practice staying calm under pressure.

9. Pray out the spirit of impatience from your life.

PRAYER POINTS

1. Father Lord, forgive me of all my doubtful and fearful life that has affected me in life in Jesus name.

2. Holy Spirit, posses my emotion and transform my attitude to glorify you in Jesus name

3. Whatever I have lost in life as a result of impatience, O Lord my God, recover them for me by your mercy now in the name of Jesus.

#28

LACK OF COMMITMENT TO PRAYER

And he spake a parable unto them [to this end], that men ought always to pray, and not to faint; Luke 18:1 KJV

When it comes to the issue of prayer, there is no argument about the fact that therein lies the power behind every great achievement on earth. In fact, beyond the pursuit of success, prayer is the link between the visible and the invisible world. It is the avenue to all spiritual resolutions, and the only route to access the maker of the whole universe. John Wesley, the great preacher once said: "it appears like God does nothing in the realm of humanity except someone prays".

Marriage being a spiritual phenomenon requires more than the physical ability to be sustained. There are forces beyond the visible realm that determine so many things about our day to day affairs; including our relational life.

In the world of bewitchment, atrocities, sorceries, witchcraft and all sorts of occultism, a Christian who handles his prayer life with levity may find him or herself a victim of the unexpected evils around.

Many happy marriages have suddenly been attacked by the wicked arrow of immorality, turning them into casualties of extramarital affairs of different sorts. To some, it is from one unexplainable sickness to the other without any medical hope. The joy of many spouses has been stolen by one demonic manipulation or the other. It is quite easier to counsel a stubborn husband or a lazy wife than to get the attention of the ones under a demonic manipulation; the only key to that is prayer.

One of the strategies of the devil against Christian marriages of this generation is to get them focused on many legitimate activities and responsibilities at the expense of their prayer altar. There is no amount of intelligence or carefulness that can replace the authority and the potency of prayer. Apostle James in his admonition states:

"Confess [your] faults one to another, and pray one for another, that ye may be healed. The effectual fervent prayer of a righteous man availeth much." James 5:16 KJV

GUIDING RULES TO OVERCOME PRAYERLESSNESS AND TO SECURE THE SPIRITUAL ATMOSPHERE OF YOUR MARRIAGE

1. Never allow anything to take the place of corporate prayer in your marriage. That's your remote control and your powerpoint for all-around victory. Whatever the case may be, a righteous and faithful prayer can resolve it.

"...the effectual fervent prayer of a righteous man availeth much." James 5:16b. KJV

2. Do not hide any accidental error or mistake from your spouse. Though it may be painful for a while, confessing it will strengthen your trust level for each other and also confirm your oneness of purpose to God.

"Confess [your] faults one to another, and pray one for another, that ye may be healed..." James 5:16a KJV

3. Never allow any grudge, bitterness or malice against anyone. It can hinder your prayers if you do. Forgive generously.

"For if ye forgive men their trespasses, your heavenly Father will also forgive you: But if ye forgive not men their trespasses, neither will your Father forgive your trespasses." Matthew 6:14-15. KJV

4. Open up every personal weakness, burden or trouble to each other and table it to God together. Remember, ***"one shall chase a thousand and two shall chase ten thousand." Deuteronomy 32:30.***

5. Ensure your family altar is a constant and lively atmosphere for the Holy Spirit to meet with you all daily.

"God [is] a Spirit: and they that worship him must worship [him] in spirit and in truth." John 4:24 KJV

6. Be your brother's keeper by checking yourselves in the mirror of the word of God always; iron sharpeneth iron.

"Examine yourselves, whether ye be in the faith; prove your own selves. Know ye, not your own selves, how that Jesus Christ is in you, except ye be reprobates?" 2 Corinthians 13:5 KJV

7. Make waiting upon the Lord a routine for both of you; either weekly, monthly or as the case may be.

"But they that wait upon the Lord shall renew [their] strength; they shall mount up with wings as eagles; they shall run, and not be weary; [and] they shall walk, and not faint." Isaiah 40:31 KJV

5 Things That Prayer Does To A Christian Marriage

1. **Connection:** A true child of God does not choose a wife or husband without contacting God for the divine choice of the right partner. Prayer enables us to connect rightly with our divinely chosen partner in marriage. And also keeps the connection until good old age.

2. **Communion:** Prayer avails us the opportunity to fellowship with ourselves regularly as humans, and with God as our Father and the Chief Cornerstone of the marriage. This constant communion in prayer and the word of God strengthens the marriage bond and connects the couples to God steadily. Little can be achieved in marriage without the weapon of prayer. The family that prays together, stay together.

3. **Confession:** Faults, mistakes and offences are easily confessed and resolved with ourselves and with God in the place of prayer.

4. **Conquering:** Prayer avails the couple the untold power to conquer every seen and unseen anti-marriage force that may be attacking the home.

5. **Control:** Just as our gadgets respond to their remote control devices, so does life respond to a praying Christian. The altar of prayer is the controlling power that rules the earth. Prayer moves the hand that holds the entire universe. Needless is the complaint and grief of an unpleasant atmosphere in the life of a praying couple. An agreement prayer of a persistent and genuine Christian couple is an irresistible pleasant aroma in heaven and a destructive bombshell in hell. It brings revelation, direction, impartation, solution and everything that glorifies God. Do you know that you can determine what happens to you and your spouse through this great weapon? If only you understand that prayer is a

major controlling device in your hand for success in marriage. A maritally informed praying couple is a potential winner in the school of marital success.

FIVE PRAYERS THAT COUPLES MUST PRAY REGULARLY

1. Holy Spirit fill my spouse afresh now for wisdom, prosperity, righteousness and all-around victory in life in the name of Jesus.

2. I take authority over the spirit of divorce, frustration and sudden widowhood now, and I decree that they shall not succeed over my marriage in the name of Jesus.

3. I take authority over the spirit of error and marital destruction assigned to target my marriage in any form in the name of Jesus.

4. Father Lord, make my marriage a living testimony of marital success in all dimension in the name of Jesus.

5. Holy Spirit, refresh, renew, and revitalize my love for God and my spouse daily in the name of Jesus.

www.ingramcontent.com/pod-product-compliance
Lightning Source LLC
LaVergne TN
LVHW040926150826
845672LV00007B/2221

* 9 7 9 8 6 5 0 9 6 7 8 6 6 *